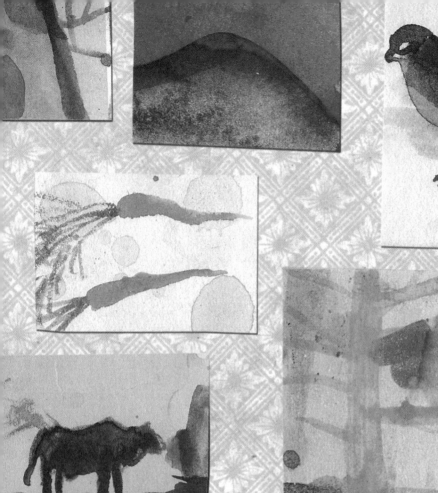

g

Groundwood Books
House of Añansi Press
Toronto Berkeley

Sara Lundberg

THE BIRD
IN ME FLIES

Translated by B.J. Epstein
Afterword by Alexandra Sundqvist

*A story inspired by the paintings,
letters and diaries of Swedish artist
Berta Hansson.*

Papa is calling again.
Calling my name, Berta,
which sounds like bird.
I pretend I don't hear.

If I fold into myself,
I look like a sleeping bird.
Like the one I made from blue clay.
I will give it to Mama.

And
if I were a bird,
I could fly off.
Away from our village —
to something else.
To a place where I could be myself.
Where no one calls for me all the time
or thinks I am ridiculous.

"You can't just sneak off like that!" Julia says.
She is the oldest, the cleverest.
Gunna, who is a year older than me, is sometimes careless.
But me — I'm hopeless.
That's what Papa says anyway.
And then there's Nisse, our little brother.
He's still small.

It's almost fall, and there is so much to be done.
We all have to help out, though Papa works the hardest.

The cows are in their summer pasture.
When Papa sends me to check on them,
I'm happy. I'm left in peace there, with the cows.
I usually take a sketch pad with me and
the charcoals I got from Uncle Johan.
Drawing is my favorite thing.
And the cows are nice and calm.
Buttercup, Daisy, Lily, Dearest.

And yet the schoolmaster wants to teach me to draw.
"Draw a carrot," he says, handing out
pieces of paper with outlines on them.
We each get an orange crayon.
"Try to stay inside the lines."
I think of the carrots in the garden
behind our house.
"Sir!" I hold up my hand.
"Our carrots don't look like this at all.
Can I draw the ones we have at home instead?"
The schoolmaster looks at me sternly.
"Don't think you're anything special."

What do things
look like?
Really?
I often think
about that.

Mama is in bed when I get home, as usual.
I put a glass of water on her bedside table.
Then I take out the blue bird and give it to her.
She looks at it. For a long time. She carefully strokes
the small cracks in the dry clay, and says,
"*Oh!* It's lovely . . . "

Mama has beautiful, kind brown eyes.
She has been ill for as long as I can remember.
She coughs all the time. We can't get
too close to her because then we could be infected.
That's what the doctor says.
I want Mama to hold me.
I want it so much that it hurts.

I go to Mama's room as often as I can.
And when Papa yells for me,
sometimes she replies,
"Daniel, let her finish drawing!"
He doesn't object then.
I imagine that all this —
the drawings and the blue clay
birds, everything I do
with my hands —
keeps her alive.
Makes her well.

No one knows how Mama got sick. It just crept up on her.
She had a fever and was tired all the time.
Then she got a cough, and the doctor said it was tuberculosis.
Horrible black spots on her lungs,
as though someone had drawn them there with charcoal.

When I was little, Mama had to go to a sanatorium,
where people with tuberculosis can rest and get fresh air.
Papa couldn't take care of me then, so I lived with
Uncle Johan and his family.

I remember that I cried for Mama. I remember that
Uncle Johan looked at me with concern, then he took my
hand and we went into a room that smelled safe
and comfortable. I almost forgot Mama when I was there.
Sometimes I was allowed to paint, but mostly I
watched Uncle Johan, who could conjure up
the most fantastic pictures.

To everyone else, Uncle Johan was just a farmer,
but to me he was a magician.

We have to be examined regularly, to make sure we
haven't become infected. The doctor says there are
billions of bacteria in a single cough.
I'm a little scared of the doctor. I wonder if he can tell
who will live and who will die.
People in the village talk about him — they say he's different.
They say that he has beautiful pictures everywhere,
painted by real artists.

The stethoscope is ice-cold. The doctor's hand is cool
and a little dry. Not at all like Papa's. Mine are sweaty.
I have to spit into a cup too, then he looks at the spit
in his microscope. After a while he says,
"Miss Berta, you are as healthy as a horse."

If I close my eyes and concentrate on feeling,
I notice a tingling in my hands. Like electricity.
Maybe that's why I like this picture
so much, the one Uncle Johan gave me.
He told me about Michelangelo,
the artist who painted it high up on the ceiling
in a church in Italy, a long, long time ago.
At first I was embarrassed because Adam
is completely naked, but now it's my favorite.
The best part is the hands.
How they *almost* touch one another.

At school, I try to copy the picture.
But it doesn't turn out well at all.
I suddenly get the feeling that God is pointing at me.
So I draw myself on a piece of paper,
cut it out and put it on top of the picture.
It looks like God is creating me instead of Adam.

A boy in my class, Olof, walks by and asks
what I'm doing. I try to explain,
but everything I say sounds wrong. Then he snatches
the picture, holds it up and shows everyone.
"Dirty Berta, who do you think you are?" he shouts.
The schoolmaster gets the class under control. Then he
tells me to put away the picture and never show it again.

"Don't worry about Olof," Gunna says.
"He probably has a crush on you . . . "
"I'm going home," I say.

When I grow up, I'm going to be an artist.
Like Michelangelo.
But I don't say that out loud.
Because it isn't a *real* job. Not something
you can be. Especially not if you're a girl.
I know that's what Papa thinks.

The blue clay is in the large gully near our house.
It feels lovely and cool and right in my hands.
You can do anything with it.
I make birds.

It's late, and tomorrow Julia is leaving.
She is almost grown up, my big sister. And now
she's going to go study home economics in a city
called Karlskoga. She's going to learn everything
about taking care of a home.
"But you know that already," I say.
She laughs.
  "Maybe, but it could be fun
      to get away and see something other
          than your little faces!"

Housewife. Housewives.
That's what Papa wants us to be —
Julia, Gunna and me —
because that's how it's always been,
and that's how it's going to be.
Maybe Julia doesn't mind,
but I don't want to.
I don't want to!

I feel a bursting and a bubbling
in my body, and I just want
to run and hide.
Sometimes I wish
I were an animal.

It's turned cold, and there's a thin
layer of ice in the gully. I can't reach the blue clay.
Maybe that's just as well, because it's hard
to sneak away now that Julia is gone.
Papa gets up first and lights the stoves.
Then he wakes me, and I have to hurry
to do the milking. If I have time, I go in
to Mama for a moment before I run to school.
She can't sleep at night.
She just coughs.

A letter from Julia arrived today.
She writes about the cinema and dances
and her new friends. Everything sounds so exciting.
I'm just about to go read the letter to Mama
when I hear the doctor's voice in her room.
I stop. I peek in and see that Mama is showing
him my drawings. The doctor looks at them carefully
and says lovely things, big words, about me.
I feel shy and warm,
so shy that I sneak away.

His words wrap around my heart like a sheepskin.
I want to tell Papa, want him to see
what the doctor sees. So I say,
"The doctor thinks I'm gifted. That I should
continue to study after graduation. Perhaps be an artist."
Papa listens, then he replies,
"The doctor knows who is healthy and who is sick,
but what my daughter should do with her life?
He knows nothing about that."

If you look carefully, you can
see Eve, hiding behind God's back.
She's waiting for her turn to come
into existence. To be seen. To come alive.
That's how it feels sometimes —
as though I too am waiting for something.
To fit in, you have to keep
your desires secret. Be silent.
And not really show who you are.

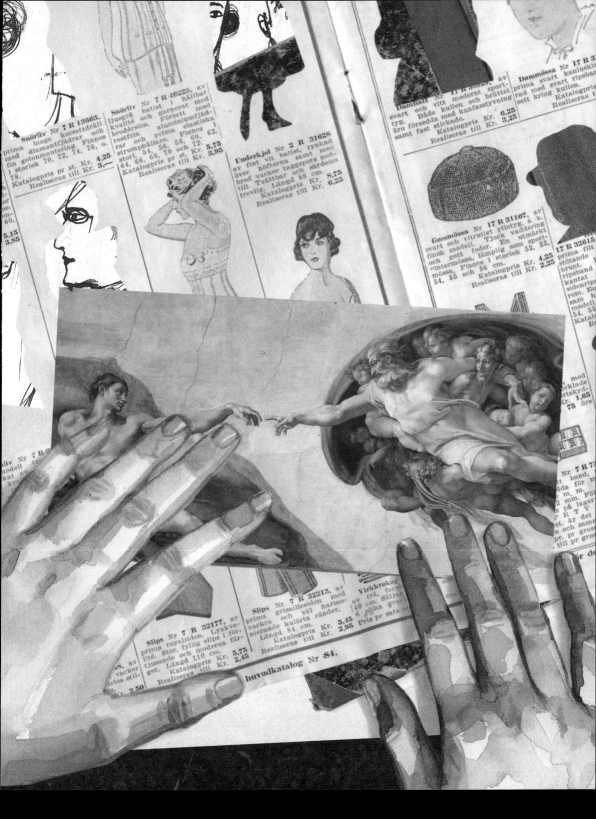

The priest reads from Genesis. It took God seven days
to create the world. On the sixth day, Adam was created.
When Adam said that he felt lonely and bored,
God created Eve from Adam's rib.
I have heard this story so many times
that I know it inside out.
Everything ends with Eve really making a mess of things.
She is disobedient and eats the forbidden fruit
and tricks Adam into eating it too.
Then everything goes wrong.
God gets terribly angry.

My stomach hurts.
Mama had a bad night again, and Papa
is completely exhausted.
Has he fallen asleep?
Sometimes he sighs so deeply that everyone can hear.

I sometimes sneak out at night, when no one can see.
I go to the doctor's house.
Not to knock on the door — I would never dare!
I peer in.
He sits in his armchair,
reading and smoking his pipe.
If he saw me, I would die.
Paintings hang on his walls from the floor to the ceiling.
They are so beautiful.
I can't stop looking at them.
To think that someone has painted them.

It is a day without shadows,
and Mama feels a little better.

She gets out of bed for some coffee.
She has dressed and done her hair.
It has been so long since I've seen her like this.
After her coffee, she takes out her sewing kit.
I struggle into my graduation dress,
so the pins don't prick me.
I drew the pattern, and Mama really wants to sew
the dress for me. She works on it
when she feels strong enough.
Now we're starting to see how it will look.
"Oh, you'll be the most beautiful girl
on graduation day," Mama says, stroking
the material.

She is just about to sew the waistband on
when she starts to cough. A deep, stubborn cough.
Suddenly blood shoots out of her mouth.
It drips onto the dress.
Gunna rushes over with a handkerchief.
"Have to rest a little," Mama manages to say,
with the handkerchief over her mouth.
We help her back to bed.
"Don't worry about your dress, Berta."
Mama's voice is weak.
"We'll wash the blood out."

Something must have broken inside her,
because a little while later more blood comes.
Dark red. Streaming. Unending.
Papa holds Mama
and gets blood all over him.
We call for the doctor,
but he isn't home.
Gunna runs for the nurse.
I can't stay in the house.

I don't know exactly when it happens,
but in the morning she's dead.
I feel it as soon as I go
into the room.
Her body is lying there,
it looks like she's sleeping.
But she isn't here anymore.

Soon Mama's room is filled with
all the people who want to say goodbye.
There is no space for me.

It is so cold that my fingers turn white,
but I don't care.
Then it comes. Silently.
It stops and looks at me.
With beautiful, kind brown eyes.

Julia comes home as soon as she can.
We clean Mama's room thoroughly.
Burn all the linens, throw everything away.
Wash and scrub. We do exactly what the doctor says.
Mama is dead, but the sickness lives on.
It might be dozing in the corner,
in the padding of the armchair
or in the rag rug.
What if it's in me?

My drawings are childish. Ugly.
The birds have dried up and come apart.
Mama is gone.
I thought that all the drawings and the clay birds
would make her healthy.
What a stupid idea.
I put them in a pile
with the other things to be thrown out.
What does it matter what I do
with my hands?

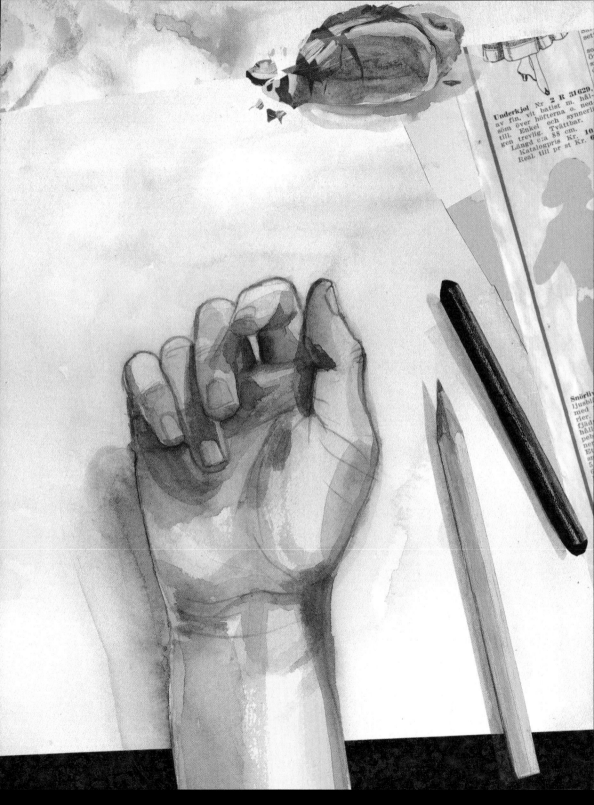

We are going to be examined again.
After Julia, it's my turn, but she takes
her time with the doctor.
What is she doing in there?
Nisse whines and fidgets.
He wants to go home.
So do I.

The paper underneath me rustles.
The doctor is concentrating.
He listens and taps.
After the examination, he asks how I am feeling.
"Fine, thanks."
"It's important to look ahead now," he says.
"People can get ill from sorrow."
"Oh." I swallow hard.
"You'll be done with school soon. What do you plan to do after that?"
I wish I could tell him about my biggest dream,
but I don't dare. Instead I say that there's a lot to do at home
and that Papa needs my help on the farm.
"You haven't considered continuing your education?" he asks.
My stomach flutters, but I shake my head.
"Papa wants me to stay here."

I don't know how much time has passed.
Just that days have passed.

Papa is out in the fields with some men from the village.
I am at the stove. The pea soup is bubbling.
Soon everyone will take a break and will come in hungry.
I ought to set the table now.
I ought to wake Nisse up and feed him.
I ought to sweep the floor.
But I'm stuck.

I close my eyes.
I see Mama.
I am little.
And she's warm.

Something snaps.
I don't know how I dare.
I know everyone will be angry.

I leave the stove, get a book
and sit down.

Before long, there's a burning smell in the house.
Someone shouts for me, but I pretend
I don't hear.

Suddenly Papa is there.
He snatches the book out of
my hands. He stands there,
shaking with anger. I ought to
say I'm sorry, but I can't.
Instead I hiss,
"I'm going to die.
Just like Mama.
I'll die
if I stay here!"

After the pea soup, nothing is the same.
Papa is so quiet.

Julia hasn't gone back to Karlskoga yet.
There's been so much to do since the funeral,
and she's had a cold.
"But after the summer, I'm leaving," she says,
pinning the waistband. It's obvious that she's longing to go.
Soon it'll be graduation.
We manage to scrub away the blood stain.
Maybe it's just a tiny bit visible.
But only if you know it's there.
There are just a few details left,
and then the dress will be done.
Julia looks at me.
"*Oh*, you'll look lovely!"
She sounds just like Mama.

I sneak away to the big gully again.
The blue clay gleams at the bottom. I dig.
The clay turns into shapes without me
deciding anything. It just does.
And suddenly there is a movement against my palms.
A little bird heart that has started to beat.
Wings that are trying to get free.
And I'm scared that I'm holding it too tight
so I open my hands . . .
Then it flies!

When I get home, I see Papa on the sofa.
He looks so old.
He's holding my drawings,
the ones I thought I'd thrown away.
Did he save them?
"Berta," he says, carefully leafing through them.
He turns to look at me.
"I've spoken to the doctor.
And it's probably not a bad idea for you to go away.
We'll manage here."

I don't know what to say.
Then he holds his hand out to me.
It is dry and warm.
I sit close to him.
He gets a twinkle in his eyes and says,
"You wouldn't be much of a housewife anyway!"

The schoolmaster has given his speech,
and now we all crowd into the schoolyard.
Papa is there. Gunna. Julia.
And Nisse.

I pick out my best drawing.
Maybe he could hang it in his waiting room?
So that whoever is sitting there, scared and worried,
has something to look at.
I ring the bell.
The doctor opens the door and looks at me in surprise.
My cheeks burn
as I hand over the drawing.
"Thank you. It's lovely," he says, looking happy.
Then he shows me in.
All the way into the living room
where all the paintings hang.

My body tingles.
I want to draw.
Get it all down on paper.
I don't want to forget anything.
To think that I'm going to leave!
It's scary. I'm a little nervous.
But it will work out.
Because I have a bird inside me
that must fly
where it will . . .

When the summer is over,
I'm going. To a new school.
A new city. To a place
where I can be
who I am.

Berta with a tripod on the hill, around 1916.

The Girl from Hammerdal

Berta Hansson (1910–1994)

BERTA HANSSON WAS in despair when she burned the pea soup on the wood stove — it was a clear protest. She wanted to get out, get away. Berta felt she had no option other than to make herself "hopeless in the household" in order to get permission to leave the farm in Jämtland county, northern Sweden.

Berta and her sister Gunna bore much of the responsibility for the household, but Berta yearned for nothing more than to explore the world outside their little village. She had begged many times to continue studying, but her father's answer had always been the same: *No, I want you both to stay here on the farm!*

While the acrid smell of burned pork and peas spread through the house, she sat reading a book. She stayed there until her father and the other men came in from their work in the fields to eat dinner and discovered "the accident."

In a rage, her father, Daniel, said she was *incompetent* — and yes, she was, by choice.

Weeks passed. Work on the farm continued as usual.

But when Berta pleaded with her father to let her continue her studies after the "ugly coup," as she called the pea-soup crisis, he changed his mind.

"And so I got away . . . " she wrote in her diary.

The incident at the wood stove in Hammerdal in 1927 changed Berta Hansson's life forever. Her quiet protest turned into a huge victory.

It was far from the norm for girls at the time to get more than a basic education. In farming communities, everyone was needed on the farm. Girls often had to do daily chores that were considered women's work until they were married off and had a new household to take care of. Even though women had won the right to vote in Sweden in 1919 (after a long political battle), they still had little opportunity to direct their own lives and careers. A girl's place was in the home, with the family.

Berta Hansson never really fit into the Hammerdal of her childhood. She carried out her daily duties, including herding the cows in the meadow or picking up scrap iron along the road to be sold for small sums of money, but she felt deep inside that there had to be another life somewhere else, a life that would suit her better.

There was a longing inside her, a longing that often drove her up the hill behind her house. She could sit there with her sketchbook for hours, gazing at the nearby farms and the Frostvik mountains, "watching the world go by," as she put it. She often

Charcoal drawing of cows, 1970s.

näst sista
dagen i inna
norrows liv, D.
ser resignerad
ut, nästan som o
dom visste. E.
Tyst klagan, K.
Imens mekan

took along a large pair of binoculars that her family had purchased at an auction.

The hill was her childhood paradise, where she played with her older sisters, Gunna and Julia. In the warmer months, it was a sea of midsummer flowers and wild strawberries. In the winter, it was transformed into a steep ski slope. Sometimes Berta climbed up the big pine tree and hid among its branches, where she read

The Hansson sisters, around 1920. Berta, Julia and Gunna.

books from the village library. She wrote, "Disconnected from all my duties and worries, I sat in my refuge . . . The world would have to manage as well as it could."

The hill was where Berta painted her first works, which formed the foundation for her later work that eventually made her one of Sweden's most important artists. She painted things in her vicinity — the landscapes, animals and people she knew well. The colors are subdued and the shapes are simple and plain. Many of her portraits depict children and are often deeply sensitive, showing their personalities and emotions.

Even as a child, Berta liked pictures, books and music. But such things were viewed as unnecessary luxuries in farming communities when she grew up. The 1910s and 1920s were hard years, marked by war and a lack of food. Wasting time on things that weren't required for the sake of survival was seen as wrong and irresponsible. Paintings were usually found only in churches, not in homes. Music was reserved for special occasions, such as family gatherings or graduations.

Berta's uncle Johan, who painted with oil paints and made fiddles and traditional Swedish *nyckelharpor* (keyed fiddles) instead of spending all his time on farm work, was disdainfully called the "theater farmer." But to Berta he was an "unusual person with exciting interests," who inspired her and influenced her choice to become an artist.

It was at Johan and his wife Nilla's home in Görvik, not far from Hammerdal, where Berta first saw a painting come to life in her uncle's hands. Görvik was where the artistic side of the family lived — her maternal grandma with her nimble piano fingers, her uncle with his love of creating. Berta too expressed her feelings by painting — "longing, pain, love and dreams."

There was sorrow in Berta's childhood. Her mother, Brita, contracted tuberculosis when Berta was born. During the first half of the twentieth century, infectious tuberculosis was a very common illness in Sweden. It was particularly prevalent among poor people and families in north Sweden, like Berta's family, who lived in crowded conditions during the long winters. In the Hansson family, Julia and Gunna became ill as well.

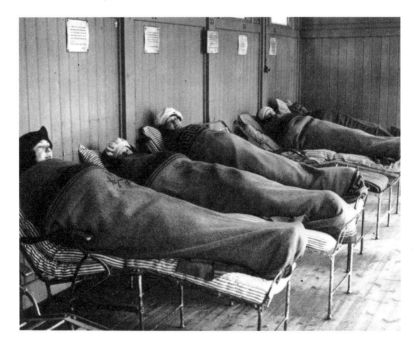

Söderby sanatorium, 1927. Between 1906 and 1910, when Berta's mother became ill, 45,578 people died from tuberculosis — 12 percent of all deaths in Sweden.

From time to time, Berta's mother stayed in a sanatorium, a sort of hospital in the countryside for those affected by tuberculosis. The fresh air was thought to improve their health.

One of the best moments in Berta's life was when her mother finally came home to the farm for good after months at the sanatorium. She could not hug her mother, due to the risk of infection. But they could have intimate bedside conversations.

"I loved and admired my mother," Berta remembered. "I thought she was the only one who understood me — my need to draw and paint."

The year before Berta left her village to continue her studies in Sigtuna, her mother died. Two years later, Berta's eldest sister, Julia, also died from the illness.

Berta Hansson knew from early on that she wanted to paint. But her path to becoming an artist was not straightforward, mainly because of the opposition she faced — the era was simply not yet ready for female artists.

Berta wanted to go to art school or train to be an art teacher, but her father firmly said no. Being an artist was no job for a woman, but she could train to teach other subjects.

"My need to tell about that little bit of reality that is mine increases every day," she wrote in her diary, when she was working as a teacher in the village of Fredrika, in the northern Swedish county of Västerbotten, after she finished her teacher training in the mid-1930s.

Throughout her years as a teacher, Berta continued to paint, during her breaks and on the weekends. The children in the simply furnished school in Fredrika become her subjects. She studied their body language, faces and emotions. She tried to paint them as they actually *were*, rather than how they looked.

In her free time, Berta devoured novels and art books. She read about famous artists such as van Gogh, Gauguin, Manet and Monet. "Everything was a revelation," she wrote. She saw exhibitions in Umeå, and tried to find friends who shared her passion for art. For a short time, she went to a painting school in Stockholm, but then returned to her work as a teacher in Fredrika.

Berta developed her own artistic language in secret. She mostly hid her paintings of the children and landscapes of Fredrika in her storage space or under her bed. But as the pile of paintings grew, so did her desire to share them with someone.

One day, seven years after Berta arrived in Fredrika, a woman stepped off the bus in the little village.

It was the author and artist Elsa Björkman-Goldschmidt, who had come to visit the school. When she entered the school hall, Elsa was amazed by a painting of serious-looking children, done in subdued colors.

"How in the world has this painting come to be here? Where did the teacher get hold of something so good?" she asked.

"I painted it," Berta replied.

She pulled her paintings from their hiding spots.

Elsa was delighted and took some of them back to Stockholm to show her friends.

Boy in a Peaked Cap, 1940s.

"I made a friend and it's unbelievable that it happened here in my village!" Berta wrote in her diary.

The following year, 1943, Berta Hansson's first exhibit opened at Färg och Form [Color and Shape], a gallery in Stockholm. The exhibition, which included sixty oil paintings, was her breakthrough.

But instead of going to Stockholm to live out her dreams of being an artist, Berta returned to Hammerdal to take care of her aging father. She felt she was needed on the farm.

When she was offered a free studio in Stockholm in 1947, she hesitated because she did not want to let her father or her village down.

She decided to stay in Hammerdal.

But this time it was her father, Daniel, who encouraged her to move.

That year, Berta also bought a train ticket to Paris, in order to experience, with her own eyes, the art she had previously only seen in books or in her imagination. She later traveled to other countries, and she lived in Stockholm until her death in 1994.

"The bird in me spreads her wings and flies where she will," she wrote in her diary.

Alexandra Sundqvist
Journalist and author,
born and raised in Boden, northern Sweden

Berta Hansson in her studio, 1990. Birds are a recurring theme in her art.

Further Reading

Berta Elisabet Hansson, www.skbl.se/en/article/BertaHansson, Svenskt kvinnobiografiskt lexikon (article by Gunilla Carlstedt).

Sources

Berta Hansson's letters and diaries (private source).

Carlstedt, Gunilla and Christian Åkerlund. *Berta Hansson*. Rimforsa: Almlöfs förlag, 2009.

Hansson, Berta. *Mina ungar. Dagbok från en byskola* [My children. Diary from a village school]. Helsingborg: LT:s förlag, 1979.

Hansson, Berta. Columns published in *Jul i Jämtland* [Christmas in Jämtland]: "Uppå källarbacken" ["Up on the hill"], 1980, and "n'Johan-mobbru" ["Uncle Johan"], 1984.

Puranen, Britt-Inger. *Tuberkulos. En sjukdoms förekomst och dess orsaker. Sverige 1750–1980.* [Tuberculosis. An illness's origins and causes. Sweden 1750–1980.] Umeå: Umeå universitet, 1984.

Statistiska Centralbyrån. *Dödligheten i lungsot i Sverige åren 1906–1910 av Kungliga statistiska centralbyrån* [Death from Tuberculosis in Sweden 1906–1910 by Statistics Sweden]. Stockholm: Statistiska Centralbyrån (SCB), 1915.

Source Notes

The quoted phrases in the afterword are Berta Hansson's own words, from her letters or diaries; the italic phrases are how she remembered her father's words. The dialogue between Berta and Elsa Björkman-Goldschmidt can be found in *Berta Hansson* by Gunilla Carlstedt and Christian Åkerlund.

Picture Sources

Berta Hansson with tripod (c. 1916) and the Hansson sisters (c. 1920). From the family's private photo collection.

Charcoal drawing of cows (1970s) and the painting *Boy in a Peaked Cap* (1940s). Photographed by Max Plunger, from the family's private collection.

Söderby sanatorium, 1927. Photo: Pressens Bild.

Berta Hansson in her studio, 1990. Photo: Stig Ström.

In the story, Berta Hansson repeatedly refers to Michelangelo's famous ceiling fresco *The Creation of Adam* in the Sistine Chapel. Photograph: Massimo Pizzotti / Getty Images.

Warm thanks to

Birgitta Larsson and Anita Olofsson
Gunilla Carlstedt and Christian Åkerlund

Published in Canada and the USA in 2020 by Groundwood Books

Fågeln i mig flyger vart den vill
Copyright © 2017 by Sara Lundberg and Mirando Bok, Stockholm
Published in agreement with Koja Agency
First published in Swedish in 2017 by Bokförlaget Mirando, Stockholm, Sweden
English translation for Groundwood Books copyright © 2020 by
Brett Jocelyn Epstein Woodstein

Groundwood Books / House of Anansi Press
groundwoodbooks.com

We gratefully acknowledge the Government of Canada
for its financial support of our publishing program.

With the participation of the Government of Canada | Canada
Avec la participation du gouvernement du Canada |

The cost of this translation was defrayed by a subsidy from
the Swedish Arts Council, gratefully acknowledged.

Library and Archives Canada Cataloguing in Publication
Title: The bird in me flies / Sara Lundberg ; translated by B.J. Epstein ;
afterword by Alexandra Sundqvist.
Other titles: Fågeln i mig flyger vart den vill. English
Names: Lundberg, Sara, author. | Epstein, B. J., translator. |
Sundqvist, Alexandra, writer of afterword.
Identifiers: Canadiana (print) 20190161035 |
Canadiana (ebook) 20190161043 | ISBN 9781773062600 (hardcover) |
ISBN 9781773062617 (EPUB) | ISBN 9781773063508 (Kindle)
Subjects: LCSH: Hansson, Berta, 1910-1994—Juvenile fiction.
Classification: LCC PZ7.1.L85 Bir 2020 | DDC j839.73/8—dc23

The illustrations were done in aquarelle, gouache and collage.
Design by Jenny Franke
Printed and bound in Malaysia

FSC
www.fsc.org
MIX
Paper from
responsible sources
FSC® C012700